One-Minute Bedtime Stories

One-Minute Bedtime Stories

by **Shari Lewis**

with Lan O'Kun

illustrated by Art Cumings

WOLF

WOLF

A YEARLING BOOK

Published by
Dell Publishing
a division of
Bantam Doubleday Dell Publishing Group, Inc.
666 Fifth Avenue
New York, New York 10103

ISBN: 0-440-40626-9
Reprinted by arrangement with Doubleday Books for Young Readers
Printed in the United States of America
November 1991

10 9 8 7 6 5

Contents

To the Parents

Picture this: Dinner's over and it's time to put your youngster to bed. The little one wants a story, and you *want* to tell your child a story. However, you are also aching to sit down with your husband or wife and establish contact once again, or collapse for a personal moment after the demands of a hectic day.

But telling your child a story is the right thing to do, so you open the book—and find yourself confronted with a twelve-page adventure of the Gingerbread Boy. Your youngster (having heard this story before) won't let you miss a single detail, and by the eighth page about the runaway cookie, you're willing to do him in yourself!

Many of our basic children's stories are well worth passing on as part of our cultural heritage. The only catch is this: These tales were written in another time, when life was lived at a slower pace, with fewer distractions and fewer available forms of entertainment. In their long form, the classic stories often don't fit our present needs.

That's why I started writing one-minute stories. And you *can* read these through in a minute, if you've had a rough day or if you're expecting ten people for dinner. On the other hand, you can stretch each tale into a five- or ten-minute shared experience with your youngster by looking at the art and asking your child "What if . . ." questions. "What would have happened if that boy had not cried, 'Wolf!' so many times before?" "What would you have done under this circumstance?" "Let's pretend that you are Rumpelstiltskin and I am the miller's daughter . . ."

In other words, this is a book that can help you satisfy

your child's needs within the context of your own busy and demanding schedule.

I find that children delight in memorizing stories. These one-minute versions are easy for even the youngest child to commit to memory. You might also encourage your youngster to retell the tales to other children in the playground or at school.

I was always fascinated by the fact that Peter Pan visited civilization to "hear the stories." The classic tales are important and even Peter Pan recognized the fact that through stories he could learn both the magical and the mundane ways in which the world works.

Shari Lewis

Rumpelstiltskin

A miller (who liked to brag) met the King. He said, "Your Majesty, I have a daughter who can spin straw into gold." So the King (who liked to have gold) locked the miller's daughter into a room filled with straw and a spinning wheel, and said, "If you can spin this straw into gold by morning, you'll be my Queen. If not, you'll die!"

The girl (who liked to live) began to cry, but suddenly, a little man appeared, and said, "If I spin your straw into gold, will you give me your first born child?"

To stay alive, the girl had to give her promise to the little man. He spun the straw into gold and disappeared.

The King, thrilled, made the miller's daughter his Queen, and a year later they had a son.

8

When the little man came to take the child, the Queen was heartbroken, and so he said, "If you can find out what my name is, you may keep your son!"

The Queen sent out a messenger who roamed the countryside and returned to the castle and said, "In the forest, I just saw a funny little man leaping around a campfire, chanting:

The Queen is in a mess
Now isn't it a shame
That she will never guess
Rumpelstiltskin is my name!

So when the little man appeared, the Queen said, "Is your name . . . Rumpelstiltskin?" That made Rumpelstiltskin so mad, he stamped his foot right through the floor and disappeared forever!

That's No Way To Do It!

Once there was a farmer who decided to sell his donkey. He placed his young son on the animal's back and they set off for town. Before long, they passed a pair of old men, who saw the boy riding and clucked, "Why is that healthy young boy riding while his poor father walks? That's not the way to do it!"

Embarrassed, the man made his son walk, and he rode the donkey instead.

Next, they passed some women who stopped working in the field to stare. They shook their heads and said, "A grown man riding while he makes his child walk! Why, he's not fit to have a son. That's not the way to do it!"

So the father lifted the boy onto the donkey's back with him, and they rode together.

But a group of children, feeling sorry for the small donkey, stopped them and said, "Two people riding on one small animal is too heavy a load. That's not the way to do it!"

So the farmer and his son both got off the donkey's back, tied the creature's legs together and slung the beast on a long pole. Then they staggered on, determined to carry the animal into town. But while crossing a bridge, the donkey squirmed, knocked them off balance, and they all fell KERPLUNK! into the river.

As they were all splashing around in the water, the farmer said to his son, "My only mistake was in trying to please everybody. There's just no way to do that, so you might as well please yourself."

The Boy Who Cried Wolf

Once upon a time packs of hungry wolves roamed the hills. This was a problem for the lone shepherds who guarded their sheep but were unable to save them when the wolves attacked. So one day, the shepherds held a meeting. They decided that, if one of them should spy a wolf coming out of the shadows, he would call, "Wolf, Wolf!" and the others would come running with clubs and noisemakers to frighten the animals away.

However, one shepherd boy thought it would be a funny joke if he were to call, "Wolf! Wolf!" during the night when everyone was asleep.

And so he did. Of course, everyone came running in their pajamas and bathrobes and nightcaps and with sleep in their eyes, all ready for trouble.

But there was no trouble. And when the other shepherds realized that they had been awakened for a joke, they grumbled a lot and shook their fists angrily at the prankster.

Unfortunately, the next night, a pack of wolves really did attack that young shepherd's flock. In panic, he stood on a high rock and cried, "Wolf! Wolf!" But the other shepherds, not wanting to be made fools of again, merely turned over and went back to sleep.

No one came to help the shepherd boy, who lost all his sheep that night because he had cried wolf, just for the fun of it.

Rip Van Winkle

A long, long time ago, in the mountain town of Sleepy Hollow, old men would get together to tell tales about the magic to be found in the mountains that surrounded them.

Among these old fellows was Rip Van Winkle. His story began on a morning many years ago, when he'd set off with his dog for a day of hunting. In a clearing in the woods, he came upon a group of tiny men with long white beards playing nine pins (which is something like bowling). They invited Rip to play, and he did.

Between his turns at rolling the ball, he joined the tiny men as they drank wine from a wooden cask. After several drinks, he fell asleep.

When he awoke, he discovered that his clothes had turned to rags, his gun was rusted, his dog was gone, and he himself had grown a beard that was so long, it fell all the way to the ground. Puzzled, he returned home only to find that his little boy had become a big man, and everyone he had ever known was either dead or grown old. Rip realized he had been asleep for twenty years!

Of course, he searched for those tiny men, but never saw them again. But when the sound of thunder echoed through the valley, he would say it was the crash of their balls striking the nine pins as they played, hidden away somewhere, high in the mountains.

The Lion and the Mouse

One day a mouse was walking
Near a lion's lair.
That's what they call a lion's cave,
He makes his home in there.

The lion sprang upon the mouse
And grabbed it in his paws.
The big cat sniffed the little mouse
And opened up his jaws.

The mouse said, "Some day, sir,
You may need a favor, too—
And if you're kind to me right now,
Then I'll be kind to *you*."

The lion laughed, "You're much too small
To be of use to me."
But on a whim, he put him down.
"Okay," he smiled, "you're free."

The little mouse said, "Thank you, sir"
And scampered out of sight.
And what do you know, the day came
When the mouse proved he was right!

For the lion was caught in a hunter's net
And he roared, "Oh, me, oh, my."
The mouse (out with the wife and kids)
Happened to be strolling by.

Seeing the trouble, he rushed to the lion,
Stood upon his paw,
Took the net in his tiny teeth,
And he began to gnaw.

In minutes, he had chewed a hole
So-o-o big, I'm telling you—
An entire troupe of elephants
Could have gotten through!

From that day on, the lion and the mouse
Were the closest of friends.
They lived happily ever after—so I'm told,
And that's the way the story ends!

Dumling and the Golden Goose

Once there was a sad Princess who never laughed or smiled, so the King, who loved her very much, said, "Anyone who can make my daughter laugh can take her for his wife." Many young men tried, but nobody could.

In that town, there was a simple boy named Dumling who owned nothing but a golden goose. One day, while Dumling was walking through town with the goose tucked under his arm, a robber tried to grab the goose. But it was a magic goose so when the robber touched it, he stuck to the goose. Quickly, the robber's friend tried to pull the robber loose from the goose, but when the friend touched the robber, she found herself stuck! A policeman tried to stop them, but he stuck to the friend!

At that moment, the sad Princess just happened to be staring out of her window when her eye fell upon Dumling with the goose under his arm, followed by the robber stuck to the goose, the friend stuck to the robber, and the policeman stuck to the friend. It was such a funny sight that suddenly, she smiled. Then, for the first time, she laughed and laughed.

Her laughter filled the castle and spilled into the throne room. When the King heard it, Dumling got to marry the Princess, and for all I know, the robber and his friend and the policeman are still stuck to that sticky golden goose.

Why the Cat Washes After Meals

As you are wondering "why" this and "why" that, did you ever think how strange it is that you have to wash your hands *before* you eat while cats wash *after* meals? Did you know, in fact, that cats wash after meals? They all do, and here's the reason why.

A long time ago, there was a polite pussycat who was proud of having good manners. One day, he caught a sparrow for his dinner.

"How do you do?" he said politely to the bird. "Please excuse me for eating you up, but I'm hungry."

He was about to pop this bird into his mouth and eat it, feathers and all, when suddenly the sparrow spoke. "My dear sir, a real gentleman does not eat without washing his hands and face. If you really were a courteous cat with fine manners, you'd wash first, too."

The cat thought about what the bird had said, and he agreed. He put down the sparrow and began to lick his paws and rub them over his whiskers. But the minute he let go of the bird, it flew away and the cat had to do without dinner.

Well, he was so mad at being tricked by that spunky sparrow, that he said, "Gentleman or no gentleman, as long as I live I will eat first and wash afterward." That is what he taught all his children to do, and that is what all cats do to this very day!

The Man Who Buried His Money

Once a man with saddlebags full of money arrived at an inn in a strange town. Afraid that someone would steal his money, he asked the owner of the inn where he could hide it.

The innkeeper suggested that the man bury the money in a dry well in the yard. "Nobody ever goes to that well," he said, "and your money will be safe."

So the man buried his money and went to sleep. But in the middle of the night, the innkeeper sneaked down to the well and stole the money himself!

The next morning the man looked in the well. He saw that his money was gone, and he realized he had been tricked. However, he was clever and thought up a plan to get his money back.

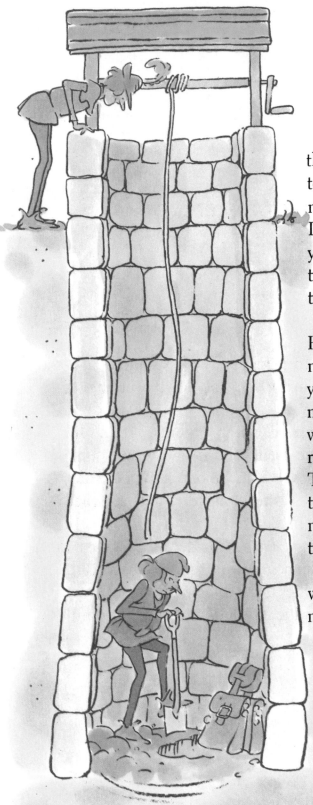

Pretending not to know the money was missing, he said to the innkeeper, "I made some more money today at the fair. In fact, I made a fortune! Do you suppose I should bury it in the same place where I buried the rest?"

The innkeeper was greedy. He wanted this new load of money too, so he said, "Yes, you should." Then he took the man's money from the place where he had hidden it, and rushed outside to the well. There he buried the money so the man wouldn't notice it was missing when he came to leave the new riches he had made.

And that night the traveler went to the well, dug up all his money, and left!

The Sorcerer's Apprentice

Once, a lazy boy was sent out to learn how to do something—anything—to make a living. Finally, he got a job working as the apprentice to a magic sorcerer.

One day as the boy was cleaning, hidden from his master's view behind a door, he heard the magician say some magic words to a broom. Whoosh! The broom sprouted arms, picked up a bucket, hopped to a stream nearby, and returned with the bucket full of water.

Not long after, the sorcerer went out to do an errand and told the apprentice to scrub the floors while he was gone. But the boy was lazy and decided he needed help. Remembering the spell he had heard, he said the magic words, and whoosh!

The broom sprouted arms. It hopped to the stream, fetched water, and poured it on the floor. Happy, the boy began to scrub the floor, but no sooner had the energetic broom dumped the first bucket out than it left and returned a moment later with another. Again, it threw water on the floor and left. Over and over again, the broom did this, and whatever the apprentice said or did he was unable to stop it.

Just as the boy was about to drown and the house to float away, the sorcerer returned. Furious, he clapped his hands and whee! The broom disappeared. The water disappeared. And the apprentice disappeared, too.

A Mouse's Wedding

Mariko, girl mouse, and Nazumi, boy mouse, were in love. However, Mariko's parents, who wanted the best for their daughter, wanted her to marry the most powerful person in all of Japan. But who was that?

Her parents looked up into the sky and spoke to the Sun. "We have a lovely daughter who would make the most powerful person in Japan happy. Won't you marry her?"

"I would," the Sun beamed, "if I were the most powerful one, but I'm not. Kumo, the cloud, is. I may wish to warm the world, but if Kumo passes before me, he can keep my light from touching the Earth, and I am helpless."

So Mother Mouse and Father Mouse approached Kumo. "Will you marry our daughter?"

But Kumo replied, "In all honesty, Kuce, the Wind, is stronger than I. A wild wind can blow a cloud like me to pieces!"

Yet the wind, when asked, sighed deeply. "I'd love to, but I'm only powerful until I hit a strong wall. A strong wall can stop my blasts and take away my breath!"

So the mice offered their daughter in marriage to the tallest wall. "I am not the most powerful one either," said Tall Wall. "Nazumi, the mouse, easily nibbles holes in my toes." And sure enough, there were some mouse holes along the base of the wall.

"Obviously, you, Nazumi, are the most powerful," said Mariko's parents. "Will you marry our daughter?"

"Yes," said Nazumi. And so Mariko got to marry the one she loved after all.

A Bell for the Cat

Once a young miller, looking for a place to do his work (which was grinding kernels of wheat into flour), came upon an old mill that had not been used in one hundred years. Finding it to his liking, he moved in only to discover that the mill was overrun with mice. They nibbled at his wheat and dirtied his flour.

So the miller bought a large cat who, each day, would kill and eat many of the small creatures. The mice, terribly upset by this four-legged new-comer, called a mass mouse meeting.

"What shall we do about this cat?" squeaked one as the meeting opened. But there was only silence until a wise old gray mouse spoke up.

"Let's put a bell around this killer cat's neck. Then, every time he moves, we'll hear him, and we'll be able to run and hide."

"Wonderful," piped another. "Let's make it a brass bell."

"Yes!" cried a fourth. "And a big brass bell at that."

"Right," squealed one more, "and let's tie the brass bell with a blue bow."

Well, you should have heard them. They all laughed and clapped and cheered—until a tiny brown mouse said, "Marvelous idea, fellows. But which one of you will hang the bell around the cat's neck?" Then there was a sudden silence, and since no one was brave enough to volunteer, the mass mouse meeting quickly broke up.

The very next day, all the mice moved away from the old mill, and neither the miller nor the miller's cat ever saw them again.

The Emperor's New Clothes

Once there was an Emperor who was very vain. Two men came to his castle one day and told him they could weave very beautiful clothing—clothing that could not be seen by silly folks but only by wise people.

The Emperor, pleased that these men thought he was a wise person, paid them lots of money to weave him such a special suit of clothes.

The men pretended to weave, but really they only moved their hands back and forth through thin air and made believe they were working late into the night. At last, they brought this so-called finished suit of clothes to the Emperor. He could see nothing, of course, but pretended to step into the pants and button up the jacket, so he would not be thought a silly fool.

Then he ordered a great parade. The people who were lined up along the streets could not see the Emperor's new clothes either, but not wanting to be thought fools, they would not admit it—until one surprised little child called out to his father, "Daddy, the Emperor has nothing on!"

When the Emperor heard the child, he knew it was true. Embarrassed, he ran all the way back to his castle, but by then the dishonest men were gone. The money was gone. And the Emperor was left with a suit of clothes that never existed in the first place.

The Baker's Daughter

Once there was a baker who had two daughters, one kind, generous, and pleasant, the other selfish, greedy, and cross.

One cold evening, the good-natured daughter was in the shop when a poor, old, ragged woman came in and begged for a bit of bread.

"Certainly, Granny," said the girl and put some dough in the oven to bake. But when she opened the door to take it out, the loaf had doubled in size.

"And so shall it always be for you, because of your generous heart," said the old woman, who was really a fairy in disguise. And from then on, everything the baker's daughter put in the oven came out twice as large.

Time went on, and one evening the ill-natured daughter was working in the shop when the same old woman came in

32

and asked for bread. Grudgingly, the girl put a tiny piece of dough in the oven, but found, when she took it out, that the loaf had doubled in size and was shiny with raisins and sugar.

"That's too large and fine for her," the girl thought and quickly hid the bread.

But the old woman, who had been pretending to sleep, woke up and asked if her bread was done.

"Bah, it burned up in the oven," laughed the girl.

"And so shall it always be for you," cried the fairy. "Henceforth, you shall say nothing but baa-baa." And with those words, the girl turned into a goat and clattered out the door.

Paul Bunyan

Paul Bunyan was the hero of many American tall tales. They say that Paul weighed 50 pounds when he was born. Do you know what you weighed at birth? I bet it was at least 40 pounds less than Paul Bunyan!

Paul was supposed to have stood 147 ax handles tall (an ax handle is about 3 feet long, so that would have made him 441 feet tall).

Since Paul was a genuine giant, he wanted to do a big job, so he invented logging. He worked his way west, clearing the forests of America so that the country had enough lumber to build homes and cities across the new land. He had many lumberjacks working for him who were huge men with gigantic appetites. They all had to be fed, so he built a cooking grill that was 24 city blocks long and 18 blocks wide. The smokestack on this stove was so tall that he had to hinge it, so that the moon could pass by. The cook had to ride a big bucking bronco to get from one end of the grill to the other, and it took a team of farm horses to pull the wagon holding the salt and pepper across the table.

Paul had 200 cooks cooking for him day and night, but they couldn't turn over enough pancakes to feed all the lumberjacks. So Paul put a piece of popcorn into each flapjack, and when they were cooked on one side, they popped up into the air and flipped themselves!

The Big Family in the Little House

Once there was a poor man who had many troubles. So he went to a wise man in the town and begged for help.

"My wife, my father, my six children, and I all live crowded together in a tiny little house. We trip and bump into each other all day, have little room to sleep, and no privacy. What shall I do?"

The wise man considered a moment, and then said, "How many animals do you have in your barn?"

"A cow, a goat, a pig, and some chickens," the man answered.

"Good. Go home and take all of the animals into the house with you," the wise man said.

The poor man was surprised, but he did as he was told. And the following day he was back.

"What a terrible thing you have had me do," he said. "The animals are into everything. They have turned the house into a dirty barn. They have eaten our food, and we have had to sleep standing up."

The wise man thought again and said, "Now go home and take the animals *out* of the house." The poor man hurried home and did so.

The next day he was back smiling. "With the animals out of the house, it seems quiet and peaceful now," he said. "And with no animals around it is so clean. And my wife and children, my father, and I have much more room in which to eat and sleep. Thank you for helping us. I'd give anything to be as clever as you are!"

Sinbad and the Genie

Sinbad the Sailor was strolling along the beach and came upon a bottle washed up on the sand. Inside was a teeny, weeny, green genie.

"Please let me out," pleaded the teeny, weeny, green genie. "I have been in here for five thousand years."

So, Sinbad pulled out the stopper and a great cloud of green smoke poured forth and grew and grew into a giant-sized genie.

"Thank you, Sailorman. And now, since I haven't eaten for five thousand years, I'm going to eat you up for breakfast!"

38

Now Sinbad was brave, but the Giant held him eight feet off the ground. And Sinbad was strong, but what could he do against a Giant? But, Sinbad was also smart—so here's what he *did* do.

He said, "Don't be silly, how can a little thing like you eat me?"

"Little?" growled the big Genie. "I'm gigantic!"

"How can you be gigantic?" said Sinbad. "You fit into that little bottle."

"I changed my shape; can't you see that?" said the Genie.

"Nobody can change his shape," laughed Sinbad.

The huge Genie couldn't stand it. "I did *so* change my shape," he said. "I'll prove it." And so the gigantic Genie turned himself into green smoke and slithered back into the bottle. Without wasting a second, Sinbad popped the stopper into the bottle and threw it out to sea to float for another five thousand years.

On Naming a Son

Once a father and a mother were arguing over what to call their new-born son. The wife wanted to name the boy after *her* father, and the husband wanted to name the boy after *his* father.

To settle the argument, they went to a judge and said, "Tell us what to do."

The judge asked the wife. "What is *your* father's name?"

"Joseph," she said.

He asked the husband. "And what is *your* father's name?"

"His name is Joseph, too," the man replied.

"Well, then," asked the judge. "What is the whole argument about?"

"*My* father was a great teacher," the woman said. "And *his* father was a thief. I can't see naming my son after a thief."

The judge smiled and said, "I suggest you name the boy Joseph and leave the rest to time. If your son turns out to be a teacher, you'll know he was named after his mother's father. If he becomes a thief, it will be clear he was named after his father's father!"

And, do you know, that's just what they did.

The Smartest Man in the Countryside

John was so clever that he had the reputation of being the smartest man in the countryside.

In the middle of the night, one time, he was awakened by a boy from the nearby inn who asked him to come quickly as there was trouble. When John arrived in the lobby, the inn-keeper said, "I've had my money stolen. Since that moment, no one has left this lobby. Do you think you could figure out which of these people did it?"

As the five people in the lobby watched anxiously, John thought about the problem.

"Get me that big old pot from the fireplace," he said, "and a rooster."

Wondering what he was going to do, they brought the rooster and the heavy iron pot, with its bottom all black with soot from the fire.

"Turn the pot upside down over the rooster," he ordered, and they did.

"Now, each of you put your hands on the bottom of the pot. When the guilty man touches it, the rooster will crow three times."

They all seemed to touch the pot, but the rooster didn't crow. There was some laughter, but John was calm.

"Now, hold your hands palms up toward me," he said.

When they did, he saw that all but one had black smudges on his fingers (from the charcoal on the bottom of the pot). John pointed to the man with clean fingers and said, "There's your thief. He knew he was guilty, so he was afraid to touch the pot!"

And that's how John came to be called "The Smartest Man in the Countryside."

The Lazy Miner

Long ago, during the gold rush days, the waters of some western rivers and streams were said to be full of gold. Hoping to get rich without working very hard, hundreds of people traveled out West to pan for gold. Scooping up mud and gravel from the streams, they would shake the wet earth and rocks through a sieve, looking for the little nuggets of gold that were said to be mixed in with the soil. As the people worked, they would tell tales about the wonderful things they'd seen.

One famous story was about a miner who was too lazy to wash his long underwear. Instead, he decided to save himself the work of scrubbing by tying the long underwear to a limb that hung over a little stream and letting it dangle in the water. He figured that the rushing water would wash it for him.

Well, one morning, the miner was too lazy even to get up and pan for gold. As a matter of fact, he was so lazy that for an entire week, the underwear just hung there and was washed by the water rushing through it.

Finally, the miner got up and remembered his long underwear. He went to fish it out —and what do you think he found?

His underwear was GOLD-PLATED!

Don't Count Your Chickens Before They're Hatched

A young woman had milked her cow and was on her way to town to sell the milk. As she walked down the path, she balanced the pail of milk on her head. It was early in the morning. The flowers smelled sweet, the sun was warm, the sky was blue, and she felt good!

As she walked, she said to herself, "This pail of milk is going to make me enough money to buy myself eight eggs. I'll take the eggs back to the farm and put them under my four best hens. In no time the eggs will hatch into eight chicks. I'll feed them the grain I harvest this fall, and the chicks will grow big and fat, and they'll lay dozens and dozens of eggs that will hatch into chickens, too.

Then I'll take all the chickens and sell them, and I'll buy myself the fanciest dress in the whole world so I can go to the nicest parties this Christmas. Then, when I get to the parties, everyone will ask me to dance, and all night long, I'll dance and twirl."

As she talked to herself, she gave a little hop and did a dance step, but when she started to twirl around, the milk pail on her head was thrown off balance. The milk was spilled and her plans were spoiled.

"Oh, look what a dumb thing I've done!" she wailed. "I counted my chickens before they hatched."